DRAGON
TALES

DRAGON TALES

A collection of short stories by
Eileen Mueller

PHANTOM FEATHER PRESS

Cover design: Jan Mueller
Cover image: Linda Bucklin
Interior art for *Rumbled*: © 2014 Geoff Popham

ISBN-13:978-1530796410
ISBN-10:530796415
AISN e-book:B019UEKRX6

PHaNtoM FeatHer PreSS

29 Laura Ave, Wellington 6021, New Zealand.
phantomfeatherpress@gmail.com
phantomfeatherpress.wordpress.com

For my special dragonets – you know who you are.

Thank you to Clarke's and Monkey Lab writers for their valuable insight.

Table of Contents

Wingspan

CHAPTER ONE – DEEP CUT

"Hey, you girls! Bet you can't jump this one!" Buzz taunts. He leaps the chasm, leaving me and Thea behind.

I stare over the edge. The chasm isn't that wide, but it *is* deep. What if I fall again? Fear churns in my second stomach.

"Don't listen to him," says Thea. "You'll be fine."

Buzz lands with perfect form, joining our classmates on the far side. All of them have jumped the gap without a problem. But they're not me.

Thea nudges me with her wingtip. "You can do it," she says.

"It's alright for you, your wings are bigger."

"But you're lighter," Thea says. "You'll make it, even with shorter wings. We'll just take a decent run up."

I gulp. "Good idea."

"Come on, Thea, Shorty," calls Examiner Longflight, stretching a kink out of his tail. "Your turn."

We skitter backwards, our talons scratching the rock. I clench mine so hard that I break off chips of stone. We run towards the chasm, leaping and spreading our wings.

My stomachs tense as we glide over the deep black gap.

Thea lands safely, yards past the far lip of the ravine.

My talons catch the edge, sending a rock clattering down the steep walls. I've made it – just. A shudder of relief runs through me. I furl my wings against my side and casually stroll over to join the class.

Buzz is crowing, "Did you see how I cleared that gap? By at least ten yards. Unlike some *shorter* attempts."

The other dragonlings snigger.

I want to tuck my head under my wing in shame, but my wings are too stubby, so I pretend I haven't heard.

Thea sticks up for me, deliberately tripping over her talons. She bumps Buzz, knocking him off-balance.

"Watch it, you fluff-ball," he growls, flicking his tail at her. Thea ducks, so he hits his best friend Aiden instead.

"Sorry, Buzz, Aiden," Thea replies, even though she's not.

"No problem, *Fluffy*," says Buzz, his eyes venomous.

Aiden's scales bristle.

"Enough fun and games," says Examiner Longflight. "Well done, Buzz. That leap was impressive. You did well too, Aiden." In Longflight's eyes, Buzz and Aiden are so good, they've practically graduated already. "Come on everyone, form up. You have to cross wider ravines before you can graduate. Let's see how you do on those." He gazes over the group, his eyes narrowing as he spots me.

We shuffle into formation and take to the sky. Although I flap furiously, I soon fall to the back. Thea joins me there, as usual.

I'm one of the oldest, but because of my

short wingspan I didn't graduate from flight school last year. I can fly, just not as fast or as far as the others. Gliding is my biggest problem – leaping over ravines and letting my wings carry me to the other side without flapping.

And today's gliding tests are the final obstacle before graduation. If I pass, I can fly with Mom and Dad in the border patrols. It's all I've ever wanted. They're the patrol's top fighters and defeated the salt pirates' last attempted salt robbery. They're the reason I got into flight academy.

"My parents discovered a new salt deposit yesterday," Thea says.

"Really?" I try to sound enthusiastic. "That's great."

If I don't graduate today, I'll become a salt miner too. I'll spend my life creeping into deep dark crevices and scratching salt with my talons, only coming out at night to fly. It's my worst nightmare.

"Buzz's dad helped them," she says. "They're heroes now too, just like your parents." She laughs. "Except they're not saving us from salt pirates, just from tail-rot, wing-mank and gizzard-gout."

She's right. Without salt, we wouldn't survive those nasty diseases. I nod.

"I mean, salt mining isn't as flashy as border patrol," Thea continues, "but it's important, too."

She knows how I feel. I don't want to mine salt beside her parents, or Aiden's and Buzz's. I want to fly beside my parents, fighting our enemies. I have to graduate. Despite what Thea says, her, Buzz and Aiden want to be in border patrol too, or they wouldn't have signed up for the academy. She's just being kind, in case I fail.

Our formation veers to the right, over the rocky plateau. Below us, dark cracks in the stone look like tiny rivers cutting through a rocky jungle, but I know they're big enough to swallow me. Some are as deep as mountains. The worst is Deep Cut, the great ravine where I crashed last year.

Thea hums beneath her breath, trying to distract me. It works.

"Hey," I ask, "why do Buzz and Aiden call

you Fluffy? It's such a weird name for a dragon."

"The same reason they call you Shorty," she replies.

Although everyone uses it, I hate my nickname. Mom tells me short wings are useful. I think she means in tight spaces like the salt mines, but I don't want to be a miner, I want to fly.

Thea looks away. "Even though I come from a mining family like Buzz and Aiden, they despise me, because I'm different."

I gaze at her sleek golden scales and long wings. "How?"

"You don't know?!" Thea flies alongside me, her eyes wide. "You haven't heard?"

"About what?"

She raises an eye-ridge. "About my scales."

"What about them? This is like twenty riddles. Can't you just tell me?"

A red glow creeps across her golden cheek scales.

"Come on. What could be more embarrassing than short wings?"

Thea's cheeks turn blazing red, like a sunburned hatchling. "My scales go curly when they're wet."

I laugh. "You're joking."

A burst of flame tells me she's not. I dive to avoid getting burned.

"Shorty!" barks Examiner Longflight. "Rejoin the formation!"

Just like he thinks Buzz is awesome, I'm sure Examiner Longflight knows I'm not. I'm the only failure in his long career as flight instructor, the only blemish on his record. Although dragonlings with other instructors sometimes don't graduate, his *always* did – until I came along. Whenever I'm near him, I feel like a dragonet-toddler after its first mud bath – dirty and in trouble.

After I failed last year, he bullied me, drilling me for hours on new wing angles until I could leap chasms. Mom told me to be grateful, but I just wanted to fly border patrol.

Flapping my short wings like crazy, I fly back up to the formation and take my position, next to Thea.

"I'm sorry, I shouldn't have got you in trouble," she says.

"And I'm sorry. I had no idea about your scales," I reply. "I guess that's why you never fly in the rain."

"Too right," she says. "And I avoid swimming. It's not worth being teased."

Examiner Longflight speeds ahead. The dragonlings follow him, long wings glimmering in the midday sun. Even though they're soaring peacefully, I flap furiously to keep up with them. At least Thea can fly as fast as the others, even if her scales do go curly in the rain.

Examiner Longflight circles down towards a huge swathe of black, scarring the rocky plateau. Deep Cut looks as if a giant has ripped the earth open with enormous claws to see what's inside. The dark bottomless pit gapes, like a toothless grimace, ready to swallow me. My wing twinges with the memory of broken bones.

Thea shoots me a sympathetic glance.

We land. My tail twitches nervously. I focus on restraining it so Buzz and Aiden can't tell how anxious I am.

Buzz puffs out his chest and strolls along

the chasm lip, his spinal ridges tall. He nears me. "Careful not to fall," he sneers quietly, so only I hear. "You don't want to hurt your *little wee wings* again."

I try to ignore him, but my knees tremble.

"Buzz, over here, please," calls Examiner Longflight.

"Sir, I was just giving Shorty a few gliding tips." His eyes are wide and innocent.

"As if…" mutters Thea.

"Thank you for being so helpful, Buzz." The examiner gestures to the yawning chasm. "You're first. Please glide across Deep Cut."

Buzz leaps high and spreads his massive green wings. They're so large, for a moment I'm in his shadow. He catches a current of warm air under his wings and soars across the dark abyss. When he lands on the far side, he roars in triumph.

"Excellent technique," says Examiner Longflight. "First, Buzz jumped high over the edge of Deep Cut. Secondly, he positioned his wings on the correct angle to ensure the thermal current lifted him over the ravine. Thirdly, he was not *afraid*." Examiner

Longflight's steely gaze rests on me.

His glare makes my knees shake harder. My tail twitches madly. So much for control.

The others notice me trembling. Aiden sniggers. Someone snorts. "Shorty's not a dragonling. Shorty's a scaredy-cat," Aiden whispers. They try to stifle their laughter.

"Enough teasing," snaps Examiner Longflight. "Everyone must graduate today." His eyes remain on me.

My scales prickle and stand on end. The thought of failing and going to the salt mines makes my knees tremble more than thinking about Deep Cut.

"You'll be fine," says Thea. "Just remember to take a good run up." She doesn't sound as convincing as before. Perhaps it's the enormous expanse of black yawning in front of us that has shaken her confidence in me. Or the stories of my crash last year.

I nod anyway. "Thanks."

"You could try leaping from that rock," she suggests.

"Against the rules. Examiner Longflight

will never let me get away with it."

The class forms a queue at the edge of Deep Cut so Examiner Longflight can call us forward to jump. Thea and I are at the back.

"Look who's coming," Thea warns.

Aiden barges past her while Examiner Longflight's back is turned and cranes his neck so his snout is in my face. "Know why we call you Shorty?" he asks. "Because you're a whole wing *short* of being a dragon, you'll fall *short* of graduating and you're on a *short* cut to the salt mines."

"Actually," I say, "they call me Shorty because I have a *short* temper." I blast Aiden with flame, but he leaps sideways, so only his facial frills are singed.

Thea grins. "Ha, ha, Aiden, your joke was *short*-lived."

Just as Aiden opens his maw to scorch her, Examiner Longflight calls him to the launch spot. "Aiden, your turn. Please show us how it's done."

Fangs bared, Aiden pretends to grin as he stalks past us. When he jumps, his majestic blue wings float across Deep Cut, far above the ravine.

Soon everyone else is on the other side. Only Thea and I stand next to Examiner Longflight.

"Good Luck," Thea calls. She runs to the edge and leaps. Her wings lift on the warm air and carry her out over the middle of the chasm where the light slants in, then across the dark shadows. Soon she's over solid ground again. She lands and roars, flapping her strong wings to encourage me.

Examiner Longflight looks me in the eye. "You can do this. I know you can. You've had a year to practice. Just remember the angle, and you'll be fine."

I nod. "Yes, Examiner Longflight. The angle."

Over the past year we'd experimented to compensate for my short wings. After hours of drilling, we discovered that if I angled my short wings differently, I could catch thermal currents more easily. In the right conditions, I could glide nearly as far as the others.

I sniff the wind. Conditions are good. Perhaps, just perhaps, I'll be lucky.

Examiner Longflight nods. "Remember, flapping is forbidden."

I run towards the edge, tense my powerful legs and leap.

I'm out over Deep Cut, the toothless grin gaping at me, jaws open and waiting. Heart pounding, I angle my wings to catch the current. A waft of warm air lifts me, sending me soaring over the middle of the chasm. The shadowy far cliff taunts me. The wind shifts. I flex my wings, angling them to catch the mellow breeze, and feel myself propelled forwards as if a team of swans are carrying me on their soft downy backs. I've never glided this easily before. Effortlessly.

Exhilaration thrills through me. The winds strengthens and blows me forward.

I hang in the air over the chasm, then land a few yards past the edge. Not once, but twice, I roar. I had no idea I could fly that far, no idea I could roar that loud. I am a short-wing and can glide.

Buzz stares at me, speechless, his snout open and his eye-ridges nearly falling off his head.

Aiden farts loudly. Thea grins. None of the other dragonlings snigger. A few congratulate me.

Examiner Longflight, who has followed me across, nods again. "Well done, Shorty. Alright everyone, there's one more chasm before you graduate."

Chapter Two – Gnasher

We form up and lift into the air. I still have to flap quickly to keep up with everyone, but I'm one of them – I can glide. A pleased rumble courses through me.

Thea flies alongside, her tail flicking with happiness as we follow our squadron.

Below I spy Gnasher – a jagged ravine, not too wide, but deadly if you crash. The sides are a series of cutthroat rocks perfect for slicing through dragon scales.

We land near the edge. "We always jump Gnasher after Deep Cut," explains Examiner Longflight. "That way, dragonlings have proven they can leap far enough not to hurt themselves here. But be careful, it's not a picnic if you miss the jump."

Thea looks worried. "Look at those sharp rocks," she says. "My uncle hurt himself here once, and nearly died."

"How can Gnasher be a problem? Deep Cut's much wider," I reply, puffing up my scales in pride. "You'll be fine."

Examiner Longflight turns to me. "Would

you like to go first?"

My chest swells. "I'm fine taking my usual spot." If I go last, they'll all be watching as I land. Buzz and Aiden will see me glide across without a problem.

One by one, the other dragonlings glide across the ravine. Thea's knees shake as she leaps, but she glides beautifully, the sun striking her dazzling golden wings. She lands, roaring.

Examiner Longflight cautions me. "Careful, the wind is changing."

Even if the wind changes, I'll be fine. I've just made it across Deep Cut. Across Deep Cut! I can do anything.

Gnasher is not so wide, so I only take a modest run up before leaping into the air. Angling my wings, I catch the warm current and drift over the ravine. Serrated teeth gleam at me from the ravine walls, ready to slash me if I fall. But I won't. I'm only yards from graduating. Nothing can stop me now.

A strong crosswind whistles along the ravine. I drift sideways. I want to flap, but remember the rule: anyone who flaps is disqualified. If I flap, the salt mines will claim me.

Panic surges in my throat, tightening it. My wings tense and shudder. Oh no, I've lost the thermal current. I re-angle my wings, hoping to catch a breeze, and am relieved when my body lifts. But it's not the soft floating lift of swans. It's more like the lift of a duckling – a quick upwards movement, a moment of hope – then I sink, plummeting towards Gnasher's teeth.

The rocky wall rushes to meet me. I furl my wings, tucking them along my body and stretch my talons out.

A gust of turbulence thrusts me against a needle-shaped rock protruding from the wall. I push against the needle with my talons and propel myself down towards the chasm floor. Air rushes past me. I land in a heap, grazing myself on sharp rocks.

Buzz's hoots ring out from above.

Examiner Longflight silences Buzz with a roar that bounces back and forth in the ravine.

"Shorty, are you alright?" His voice sounds

distant.

"Yes sir. I'll be up soon."

Clambering to my feet, I evaluate my options. I could walk out, but the ravine seems to stretch forever. Who knows where the end is? I can't flap, or I won't graduate, so flying up is not an option. The sharp rocky walls have plenty of foot holds, so I could climb up. My compact body and small wings mean climbing is easier for me than for long-winged dragons. I decide to climb.

The rocks dig into my talons and legs, drawing blood. When my legs are not long enough, I use my jaws to lever myself higher. It's an acrobatic feat to reach some of rocks. I clamber sideways more than upwards, making slow progress.

Examiner Longflight and Thea shout encouragement down to me.

With only a few yards to go, I emerge from the shade, with bloodied talons and cuts all over.

The examiner roars, "You're nearly here! Keep going."

Perhaps he does like me, after all. Maybe all

those drills last year weren't bullying. Maybe they were to help me, like Mom said. I climb towards him.

He reaches down with strong forelegs, hoisting me onto the plateau. I slump on the rock, gasping, too tired to care what the others think. None of it matters any more. I couldn't glide across Gnasher. As soon as my cuts heal, I'll be working in the salt mines.

I close my eyes. Sun beats down on my body. I wait for the jeers, the catcalls and the rude comments. But the other dragonlings are silent.

"Off you go," calls Examiner Longflight. "Shorty's alright. I'll see the rest of you at the graduation feast tonight."

Thea nudges me with her nose before she flies off. Was this the last time I'd fly with her? Maybe not. Maybe I'll fly with my friends and family now and then. Not that I have any other friends to fly with. A tear runs down my scales into my mouth, its salty tang startling me. Salt – my future, my life. It's enough to make a dragon cry. But I'm not a real dragon. I'll never be on border patrol.

Examiner Longflight settles on his haunches beside me. He places his wing over my aching body. "Shorty."

I open my eyes.

"I've sent them away, but not until they'd seen your bravery in climbing out. You were clever and courageous, and it saved your life. Not many dragons would have bounced against the rocks like that." His eyes shine with pride. "But I'm not sure if it's enough to graduate. Only the chief examiner can decide."

"What? I thought I'd failed."

"You didn't flap, so there's a chance she'll let you graduate for being creative in a tricky situation. I'm not sure if it's enough to qualify, but we can try."

"Thank you, sir."

"Don't get your hopes up." His face is so grim, my hope evaporates like steam off a newborn hatchling in summer.

CHAPTER THREE – SAPPHIRE LAKE

We make our way back to the dens, passing the other dragonlings basking on the rocks by the sparkling waters of Sapphire Lake. Dragonets frolic in the shallows, their parents nearby. My muscles ache and my cuts throb, but the pain is nothing compared to my stinging pride. I want to fly away and hide, but Examiner Longflight stops me, his wingtip touching my shoulder.

"Face them. Be proud of who you are."

I raise my head, meeting my classmates' stares.

Aiden's eye-ridges pull down as his gaze slides over my wounds. Buzz's lip curls and he glances away. Only Thea smiles, but it's tinged with sadness.

An orange dragonet, leaping among the rocks, pipes up, "How did Shorty get hurt?"

"Be quiet, Spiky!" his mother hushes him.

Examiner Longflight clears his throat. "Let's find your parents."

No, not Mom and Dad. I've failed. I don't want them called off border patrol, just to see me like this. "Um, could I have a little time to myself?"

His eye-ridges pull into a deep frown. "I'm not sure if–"

"I promise I'll see them before… um …the feast." I can't say graduation. It sticks in my throat.

"I guess that'll be fine. Meanwhile, I'll see the chief examiner." Examiner Longflight takes to the skies.

With a thump, Thea lands beside me. "Are you alright?"

"Although I'm going to miss you, right now, I want to be alone."

"But–"

"Please!" Slinking behind the rocks, I drag my tail along the ground until I'm far away from prying eyes. I slump onto the hard stony surface, sighing. My nose is inches from a crevasse. I close my eyes against its dark shadow and drift to sleep in the sun.

Whump! Something lands on my tail, waking me.

It's Spiky, the orange dragonet. "Tell me how you got hurt, Shorty."

"It's nothing. Go away." Resting my chin on the rock, I gaze at the crevasse. It's as dark as my future mining salt.

"Mom says it's rude to ask, but I'm curious." Spiky leaps off my tail and bounces along the stony ground until he's right in my face. "Want to play?"

"What are you doing here? Go back to the lake where it's safe."

"Please play with me," Spiky pleads.

"No." I shut my eyes. Maybe he'll get the hint.

He pulls one of my eyelids up. "You're not really sleeping," he announces.

I shoot a warning flame past his snout. It expires in a puff of smoke, leaving his face sooty.

"Spiky!" The bellow shakes the ground.

"Oops, that's Mom." Spiky scampers off, leaping over rocks near the lip of the crevasse.

His mother swoops down, talons outstretched, the shade of her vast wings suddenly cooling me. As she's about to nab him, Spiky dances out of reach and tumbles into the narrow chasm.

A thump cuts off his shrill shriek.

I scramble to the edge and peer over.

"Help me!" Spiky is on a ledge halfway down.

His mother dives at the narrow opening, but her wings hit the edges. She roars in frustration, her scrabbling talons dislodging a shower of rock.

"Ow, that hurts," Spiky's high voice echoes up.

Don't worry, Spiky," his mom calls. "We'll get you out." She lifts her head, and bellows, summoning the patrol.

Roars and flapping fill the air. Dragons land. Dragonlings too. Everyone comes to see what the emergency is.

"I can't fit down the gap." Spiky's mom tries again, but her wings bash the edges.

I think I'm small enough to rescue him. "I'll fit," I call, but no one hears – except Buzz.

Buzz shoves me aside and struts forward. "I'll go!" he booms. Leaping into air, he dives towards the crevasse. One of his wings smashes against the ground and he crashes onto the rocky plateau, moaning. His wing is bent at an odd angle.

"I'll fit," I say, louder this time. Everyone turns to me.

Thea calls out, "Shorty's the perfect size."

Examiner Longflight nods.

At the back of the crowd, my parents are watching. A lone dragon circles above us. Everything is silent, except for Buzz's moaning.

"Oh, shut it, Buzz," snaps Aiden, making him stop.

The crevasse is too narrow for a run up. Too dangerous to dive into. I slip over the edge and drift downwards. It's tight, but my wings just fit. A collective sigh comes from the dragons, rustling through the ravine like wind through leaves.

I glide down.

"Shorty, it's you!" Spiky cries, huddled on the ledge.

Snatching him in my talons, I fly up to the crowd, and place him at his mother's feet. She settles on the ground and curls her body around him, her wing sheltering him. A pleased rumble issues from her throat. She gazes at me. "Thank you."

Roars of approval ripple through the crowd.

The dragons move to make space for a huge brown dragon to land.

It's the chief examiner. She faces me. "Examiner Longflight spoke to me of your resourcefulness. I'll admit, I wasn't convinced. But after seeing you rescue Spiky, I've changed my mind." She lowers her nose and nudges Spiky before continuing. "Your short wingspan has come in handy today. No doubt we can use your climbing skills as well. Not only are you clever, you're brave."

"Me? Brave?"

She nods. "For years, we've watched you struggle with ridicule and your physical limitations. We've wanted you to succeed, to graduate, and to see that your differences are a talent, not a weakness. Today, you demonstrated your unique abilities. You will graduate with the other dragonlings tonight."

A thrill runs through me. "Yahoo," I trumpet, "I'll be on border patrol!"

Thea leads a cheer and everyone joins in, roaring. It hurts my ears, but I can't help grinning.

Buzz meets my gaze squarely, new admiration in his eyes. Aiden nods, as if he approves.

With roars and the flapping of wings most of the dragons and dragonlings fly back towards the nesting dens. Buzz and Aiden walk, Buzz cradling his bruised wing against his side. Spiky's mother calls goodbye as she flies home, cradling her sleeping dragonet in her talons. Only Mom, Dad and Thea are left.

Mom nudges me. "I told you short wings could be useful."

Dad chuckles, a deep rumble making his scales quiver. "Well done. Very well done. We're proud of you."

"We always are." Mom winks, then looks over my cuts and bruises. "A swim in Sapphire Lake would help ease the pain. We'd better get back to patrol duty."

"Thanks, Mom. You too, Dad."

"See you tonight," Mom calls as they leap into the air.

Thea nudges me, "I'll come for a swim too," she says, "even though my scales will go curly."

I grin. "That'd be great, Fluffy."

"Yeah, Shorty, I think so, too." She dives into the water, splashing me.

For the first time, my nickname doesn't sting. I flex my short useful wings, and water droplets sparkle on them, like diamonds, in the sun.

Fluffy's Triumph

Note: This story is an epilogue for Wingspan, so to understand *Fluffy's Triumph*, you should first read Wingspan on page 9.

The cool water of Sapphire Lake flowed over Thea, sinking into the spaces between her scales and soothing her dry hide. As her scales got wet, they prickled, curling and standing on end, allowing the water to calm her itchy skin. Aah, this was bliss. It'd been so long since she'd swum. She'd given up after Buzz and Aiden had called her *Fluffy* because of her wet curly scales. Thankfully they weren't here to tease her. Thea stayed in the lake for ages, diving deep and surfacing to spray Shorty.

Shorty got out of the water and sat on the rocks, sunning. She unfurled her wings and stared at them as if she'd never seen them before. Thea guessed she hadn't. Not like this. Shorty's wings hadn't ever been useful or beautiful – until today. Now, everyone admired Shorty for saving Spiky, a silly dragonet that had fallen in a crevasse. Perhaps – now that Shorty was a hero, despite her tiny wings – Buzz and Aiden would accept Thea's curly scales too.

Smiling, Thea climbed out and joined her friend on the rocks. They still had an hour or two until they graduated from being teenage dragonlings to becoming real dragons.

Shorty looked up and laughed. "Look at you, Thea. Your scales are really curly. They stick out so much, you look twice your size. They make you huge and ferocious."

"Ferocious? You're joking." She'd been teased so often about being fluffy, the last thing Thea expected was to look fierce.

"No, really, they make you look so large and scary. You should have kept up your swimming. You probably would've terrified Buzz and Aiden."

They laughed.

"That would've served those bullies right." Thea held out a foreleg. "I agree, my leg does seem a lot larger than usual."

"And that's just your leg," Shorty said.

"Seeing all of you is pretty terrifying."

"I don't want to be scary," Thea said. A flash of orange in the nearby rocks caught her attention. "What's that?"

Shorty rolled her eyes. "I bet you a sack of salt that it's Spiky. He's probably finished his afternoon nap and is out being nosey again."

"I'm not nosey!" Spiky's head popped up from behind a rock. "I'm just–" He looked at Thea. "AAAGH!" He ducked behind the rock again.

"Told you so, Thea! You *are* scary." Laughing, Shorty snatched up the trembling dragonet with her talons. "You're going home, Spiky. And then, you're staying there." She flew off with Spiky protesting loudly.

Thea sighed. She'd thought being fluffy was bad, but being terrifying was worse. She liked playing with dragonets, not scaring them.

But if she was going to be scary, she may as well enjoy another swim. She dived back into the lake and swam to the other side, getting out near the salt storage caverns. Over here, she was unlikely to startle any silly dragonets.

Stretching out on a high flat rock, Thea surveyed the salt caverns. That was odd – there were usually guards outside, but today no one was here. Perhaps they were helping prepare the graduation feast. She smacked her lips. When she was dry, she'd go and help too. There might be a delicious morsel or two to spare.

Out of the corner of her eye, something green slithered between two rocks. Another curious dragonet? Thea slipped off her rock, hiding behind it, so she wouldn't scare the little toddler.

What was a dragonet doing so far away from the clan? It could fall in a chasm like Spiky and get hurt. She really should keep an eye on it. Peeking around the rock, she saw another green form slithering nearby. Its long jaws and stubby legs disappeared behind a boulder, followed by a whip-like tail. Dragonets didn't slither. And they didn't have stubby legs or whippy tails.

Salt pirates! Their salt caverns were being raided!

And the guards were gone.

Without salt, the dragon clan would suffer tail-rot, wing-mank and gizzard-gout. Dragon hatchlings would die. Elderly dragons would grow weak and ill. Thea's scales – already curly and sticking out because they were wet – stood out even more in rage. She charged out from behind the rock, flying directly over the salt pirates, and roared as loudly as she could. The rocks near the cavern were seething with them. At first they ignored her, until one glanced skyward and let out a screech of terror.

"Monster!"

They all stared up at her. Shrieks filled the air. "Salt demon."

"Run!"

"Flee! Raid cancelled."

Thea roared again.

Slithering writhing bodies burst from behind the rocks, speeding away from the salt storage cavern. The salt pirates scattered as the border patrol arrived in answer to her roars. The patrol flamed the pirates' cowardly tails and chased them out of dragon territory.

Shorty's dad remained behind with Thea.

"We heard your cry, Thea. Are you alright?" He eyed her scales.

"There were no guards," she replied, "so I had to scare the pirates."

"More salt pirates attacked the far border," he said, "so we called the guards to help us defeat them. Those crafty pirates must've been creating a distraction so this second team could steal our salt."

Shorty returned, landing beside them. "What happened, Dad?"

"Thea saved our precious salt from the pirates. She's saved us from tail-rot, wing-mank and gizzard-gout. And she scared those pirates single-handedly." He placed a proud wing across Thea's back. "Both of you are heroes today."

"Then let's feast!" said Shorty. "The graduation ceremony is beginning any minute."

"One moment," Thea said, diving into the water again. She surfaced, laughing. "I want everyone at the ceremony to see my terrifying curly scales. Especially Buzz and Aiden!"

Suds and Scales

"Get in that bath," Mom insisted. "You're dirtier than a worm in a mud puddle and smellier than dad's gym shoes."

I stomped into the bathroom and slammed the door. What was wrong with a bit of dirt? It was all natural, no additives and definitely no refined sugar – another thing Mom was always going on about. I was only going to get dirty again tomorrow.

Peeling off my sweaty socks, I tucked them in the cabinet behind the shampoo, instead of in the hamper. Hopefully Mom wouldn't sniff them out – I only had one pair of socks in my team's color and I needed them for my football game tomorrow.

Mom rapped on the door. "I can't hear the water running."

Sighing, I turned on the faucet.

"Use soap," she called. "No cheating."

I tipped some liquid soap into the bath. Soap was evil, but if I had to use it, I might as well have bubbles. When the water was deep and sudsy, I dumped my clothes on the floor and got in. Wrinkling my nose at the floral stench, I looked down. There were so many bubbles, I looked like a corpse-less ghost, or an alien with froth for a body.

"It's not fair," I moaned. "Why should I have to wash every day?"

The toilet seat clunked.

I turned so fast, a mini tsunami sloshed onto the floor.

Nothing was there – except the clothes I'd dropped and the water I'd spilt. Nothing that could've made the toilet clunk. And now my underpants were swimming happily in the aftermath of my tidal wave.

I lifted my right knee above the water and scrubbed it with the washcloth.

Clunk!

I whirled back. Oops, another flood.

Before my eyes, a long claw slid between the toilet seat and lid.

My heart thudded, like I was running for

goal.

Two more claws reached over the edge. A scaly limb slithered out and flung the lid open with a crash. Another taloned limb grasped the seat. With a grunt, a dripping head emerged from the toilet!

"Whoa!" I yelled, as a little dragon clambered out and perched on the seat. It was green with baby-blue eyes and had an odd crest sticking up on its head. Luckily I had lots of bubbles or that dragon would have seen too much.

"I heard you yell," called Mom. "What's going on in there?"

Mom would really flip out if she saw this little guy. "Ah... I dropped the soap. That's all."

The dragon shook itself like a dog, spraying droplets everywhere. Dribbles splattered the mirror, ran down the walls, and landed on the towels. Yuck! Germy toilet water was all over the place. I eyed my towel on the rail. I'd have to remember to get myself a fresh one.

"What are you doing?" the dragon's voice was tiny.

Had I heard right? Had it really spoken? "W-what did you say?"

"What are you doing? Is it fun?"

"Well, I'm getting clean, and no, it's not fun. I hate it."

"What's that foamy white stuff? Does it taste good?"

"Depends if you like roses." I picked up a handful of bubbles and blew them over the floor.

"I don't know if I like roses." The dragon leapt off the toilet, pouncing on the foam, its talons slithering across the slippery tiles. Its feet got tangled in my clothes, sending it tumbling. My undies flew up in the air and, as the little critter sat up, landed on its head. What a sight: baby-blue eyes peeping through the leg-hole of my dripping undies, its wee dragon body covered in soap suds.

"That was fun," the dragon said, and leapt into my bath, the undies floating away.

"Aagh!" I jumped out, skidding on the floor, and landed in the mess. "No way, little guy. You're dirty! You've been swimming in the grubby toilet." I snatched my towel to cover my private parts, then realized, too late, that my towel was damp – with toilet water!

Rummaging in the cupboard, I dropped the filthy towel and tugged a fresh one around me.

The dragon was diving in the bath and thrashing among the soap suds, flinging bubbles around the room with its tail. "Can we play together? Are you coming back in?"

"But you've been in the toilet."

It cocked its head. "Did you want to swim in the toilet too? There's no foam, you won't fit very well and the water's colder. I like this warm water much better."

"No, that's not what I meant. The toilet is germy, so you're dirty. You really need to wash."

"Dirty? What's that?"

"It means… never mind. You have fun in there for a few minutes." I had to get the smelly toilet germs off me. I couldn't get sick and let my team down tomorrow. Turning on the shower, I got in. Luckily the glass was frosted, so the dragon didn't have a million-dollar view of me. I grabbed the soap and lathered it all over my body, scrubbing hard with a washcloth to make sure those germs were gone.

A small voice piped up, in the air above me. "Why is it raining inside?" The flying dragon tilted its head to stare at the ceiling. "There are no clouds in here."

Except the thunder cloud over my head. How dare that pesky dragon peep while I was showering? The lathered soap protected me from view, but I used the washcloth too, just in case.

The dragon spied the shampoo bottle and bit it, squirting shampoo all over the shower walls.

"Hey!" I squealed.

"Sorry," it yelped, and flew out of the shower, diving into the bath . A huge plume of water shot up, splashing the floor. Not again. There was enough water out there for an Olympic swimming event. Even enough to wash a dirty football team.

I scraped dribbles of pearly shampoo off the glass, collecting them in my palm. What a waste! Might as well use it. Mom would go nuts if all the shampoo was gone and I still had dirty hair.

In the middle of working the shampoo into my hair, those baby-blue eyes peeped over the top of the glass again.

"Would you wash my crest too?"

"Sure, in a minute." That little dragon needed a thorough scrub all over to get rid of those poo-ey germs.

Mom knocked at the door. "Are you going to be much longer?"

The dragon dive-bombed the bath, splashing the walls and soaking the other towels on the rail.

"Are you using the shower and the bath at the same time?" Mom sounded way too curious.

I had to think fast. "I was so dirty, I need to shower *and* bath today."

"At the same time?"

"Um… yeah. I'm scrubbing myself in the bath then rinsing in the shower."

"Okay." She sounded doubtful. "Remember to wash your hair."

"Already done," I called.

"Fantastic!" She sounded surprised. "But not too much longer, I still need some hot water for my shower."

I breathed a sigh of relief as Mom's footsteps went back down the hall. Drying myself, I pulled on clean underwear, shorts and a T-shirt from a hook on the back of the bathroom door. Luckily they were still dry.

But not for long. The dragon's next splash soaked me from head to foot – with its filthy bathwater.

The dragon sat on the edge of the bath, its tail trailing in the water. "Will you wash my crest now?"

"Only if you stay there and don't move while I get everything ready."

The baby dragon bared its fangs and tugged its lips up. It was smiling – the weirdest but cutest smile I'd ever seen.

I pulled the plug out of the bath. The water – now an odd shade of brown – went down the drain with a huge slurp.

The dragon twitched, its eyes round. "Will it swallow me?"

A long exaggerated sigh hissed from my

lips as I eyed dripping walls, shampoo smears, soaking towels and the ocean I was standing in. "Stay right where you are and you'll be fine."

The dragon froze on the edge of the bath, looking more like an ornate dragon fountain than an animal. I could imagine water spouting from its mouth at any moment.

I ran more warm water into the bath. When I turned around, the dragon was balanced on the toilet seat, drinking water from the bowl.

"No. Don't! It's dirty!"

"There's that word again. What does dirty mean?"

"It means that water may make you sick."

The dragon's eyes widened in alarm. "I don't want to get sick."

"Here, I'll help you." I grabbed my toothbrush and toothpaste and cleaned the dragon's fangs. "You have to take care of your health," I said. "You can't just drink any old water." I rolled my eyes – I sounded just like Mom.

I turned off the bath faucet and, when I

looked again, the dragon's tail was curled around my toothbrush. It stamped on the toothpaste tube to squeeze out some more.

I laughed, until it flew towards me, toothbrush still in its tail.

Clamping my mouth shut, I turned my head away, so the dragon couldn't brush my teeth with the grubby brush it had just used for its *toilet-water-drinking* teeth.

"I'm fine, thanks. You can keep that brush. It's a gift, just for you." I grabbed a new brush out of the cabinet, hurriedly smeared it with what was left of the toothpaste, and brushed my teeth.

The dragon brushed its fangs. Afterwards, I put my new brush safely in the cabinet, so it wouldn't end up in the dragon's clutches.

Then I popped the dragon in the bath and soaped it well. I even shampooed its crest. I scrubbed the creature's hide with a soft nail brush. It purred happily, turning a lighter shade of green. The water turned dark gray, not clean enough for rinsing.

Pointing to the shower, I said, "Fly around in the rain for a while, while I clean up."

I used the wet towels to mop up the floor and walls, and rinsed the shampoo off the shower walls. Then I gathered all the sopping gear and dropped it into the bath with a satisfying squelch. The dragon flew out of the shower, rubbing its body against a freshly-hung towel, then flitted around the room. I tossed its towel into the bath, too.

I was still damp, but the bathroom was cleaner than before.

A deep rumble issued from the toilet. The dragon's eyes shot wide open. "Ooh! That's Mom calling me for dinner!" It perched on my shoulder and gave me a minty-toothpaste kiss! "I'll be back tomorrow, so we can play again." It grabbed my old toothbrush in its talons and dived into the toilet with a splash.

I dashed over and peered into the bowl. There was nothing there.

Mom knocked on the door. "Did you hear that thunder? I think there's a storm brewing."

"I'm done. You can come in."

She opened the door and her jaw fell open. "Oh! You're clean! And you've cleaned up after yourself. You've done such a good job, I'll make you a hot chocolate."

"Um, I've already brushed my teeth."

Mom was speechless, except for a quiet, "Wow." She swept the towels and dirty laundry out of the bathtub.

"Oh, Mom, I think you forgot these." I reached into the cabinet and took out my smelly socks. "I'll need them for my game tomorrow."

"Thanks," she said, her eyebrows raised, as if she couldn't believe her luck. "I'll do the laundry right away." She marched out, leaving a trail of drips behind her.

Outside, thunder rumbled through the sky. Was that what I'd heard? Or had there really been a dragon growling in the toilet, a moment ago? Maybe I'd imagined it. Mom was always telling me I had an over-active imagination. As I left the bathroom, I picked up a washcloth Mom must've dropped. Something wet glinted against the fabric. I looked closer.

It was a green scale.

Dad's Wisdom

The dragon's eyes were burning embers in the dark, making its green scales gleam. It licked the white tips of its fangs, grinning at me from under my bed. It was hungry.

Heart pounding, I reached for my lunchbox.

I fed the dragon stale crusts and left-over apple cores, but it wasn't satisfied. Over the next few days I stole biscuits, then loaves of bread, and even dropped chunks of meat into my pockets at dinner to smuggle up to my room – desperate to keep the dragon's hunger away so I could sleep.

When I told Dad about the hungry dragon, his advice was simple. "Hang your toes off the edge of the bed and he'll nibble your toenails. You won't have to cut them and the dragon will be fed. That way, you'll kill two birds with one stone."

Dad's advice was perfect, although I couldn't kill two birds with one stone. In fact, it took quite a few stones just to kill one bird – but after eating it, the dragon was quiet for two weeks.

Although Mum wasn't. "Stupid cat left feathers under your bed. It's a pest, killing lovely birds like that."

Dad agreed. "Maybe we should get rid of it."

When the dragon's stomach grumbled, I took Dad's advice again. The dragon gave an appreciative rumble as the cat's tail disappeared down its jaws. This time I waited until the dragon was asleep, quickly whisking the broom under my bed to clean up the fur balls before Mum got home.

I took care to sleep in the middle of my mattress, making sure my arms and legs didn't dangle off the edge. For over a month, the dragon was silent as it digested the cat. I smiled and laughed. I even dared to invite my friends over again.

Bobby came to play and crashed my bike, bending the frame beyond repair.

"He's such a menace," said Dad. "Someone should do something about him."

That night the dragon awoke. It's roars shook my mattress. It was desperate to be fed. Flames licked out from under my bed. I sat sweating, hunched with the blankets wrapped around me. I didn't dare sneak out until after dawn when the dragon was quiet.

Later that day, I convinced Bobby that the best place for hide 'n' seek was in my room – under the bed.

We never did find him. His shoes turned up at the local playground, puzzling the police for months. Bobby must've been extra nourishing because the dragon was quiet for a year.

When it awoke from its digestive slumber, it became demanding, begging for food all through the night, nipping at my ankles as I leapt into bed – a warning that it could gobble me up if I didn't bring it something large to eat. After smuggling bread, fruit, tuna, and even chocolate into my room, I finally decided to ask Dad what to do.

He was in the kitchen, staring at the

grocery receipt. "What on earth have you been eating?" he asked, shaking his head. "Our grocery bill has doubled! How can I pay this? You'll be the *death* of me!"

His advice, as usual was good.

I'm sure going to miss it.

(This story was adapted for children from *Dad's Wisdom,* which was first published in *Baby Teeth*, Paper Road Press 2013 – a collection of stories for adults, which raised funds for Duffy's Books in Homes: a New Zealand charity for children's literacy.)

Math Dragon

"Sean McIntosh!" Miss Hanson roared, her fiery-red hair nearly standing on end.

I yanked out my math book, but it was too late. She stalked down the row of desks and snatched it up, uncovering my rubber band and spit-balls. Glancing around the classroom, her eyes took in the white blobs stuck in Sarah's curly hair.

Luckily Miss Hanson couldn't see the two paper balls stuck to the back of her fluffy sweater – like baby possums clinging to their mother. The kids behind her sniggered, pointing at her back.

"Spit-balls? Disgusting!" she said, sweeping my ammo into the bin. "I warned you, Sean. Move your desk to the back corner."

The other kids grew silent, even Jack and Luapo. There was no farting, eye rolling, or sniggering.

"But I–"

"For the whole week!" Miss Hanson glared. "If you play up again, I'll send you straight to Mr Grinchov to work in the garden."

Sighing, I dragged my desk to the corner – the drafty musty-smelling corner near the cloakroom, miles away from everyone.

Jack and Luapo ignored me, heads down over their work. Traitors. They'd suggested firing spit-balls. It wasn't fair.

"Focus now, class." Miss Hanson's pen squeaked sums onto the whiteboard.

I opened my desk to nibble my chocolate cake while Miss Hanson wasn't looking – and nearly fell off my chair. A large orange lizard sat on my books among chocolaty crumbs and smeared icing. No, it wasn't a lizard! It was a baby dragon, with yellow eyes bright against orange scales.

It burped. "Hi, I'm Bob."

A talking dragon? Named Bob? "What?!"

Miss Hanson heard me. "Sean, did you have a question?" she snapped.

I slammed my desk shut, wishing I could

pick the spit-balls off her sweater. I was going to be in more trouble when she got to the staff room and someone pointed them out. "Um, just looking for a pencil."

"Do it silently." Miss Hanson scratched her arm. Her skin was so dry it was nearly scaly.

"Yes, Miss Hanson."

"The rest of you may help each other. Call me if you're stuck."

Great. Math alone – without help. I ducked my head and looked at my work. "Sixty-four divided by eight is..."

"Eight," whispered Bob.

"Nine times seven?"

"Sixty-three."

As soon as everyone was talking, I opened my desk. It wasn't my imagination. It really was a talking dragon. A dragon that was good at math. I couldn't believe my luck!

"What are you doing in my desk?" I whispered.

Bob's tongue flicked over his fangs, licking the icing off my books. Crawling onto my green pencil case, his scales became green. "I'm hungry," he said, twitching his tail, the tip turning red to match my exercise book.

"Wow, how did you do that?"

"Coloration crypsis."

"You *what*?"

"It's how I change color. It's useful when I'm hiding." His scales turned orange. "This is my favorite color." Craning his head out of the desk, he sniffed me. "Do you have anything else to eat?"

"Nothing here." I shrugged. "Well, my lunch is in the cloakroom. Hey, where are–"

Bob had jumped out of my desk, turning carpet-grey and dashed behind me, making a beeline for the cloakroom.

Strange rummaging and munching drifted out of the cloakroom. No one else was close enough to notice the odd sounds, but they distracted me from math. Miss Hanson was at Amanda's desk, busy helping her, so I sneaked out to take a look.

Bob wasn't there, but the floor was covered in half-eaten food. I whipped back to my desk, and kept my pencil busy in my book. But not busy enough.

Miss Hanson loomed over me. "Sean,

you've only done five of twenty equations. You'll have to stay in during morning break to finish."

The bell rang. Kids rushed to the cloakroom.

"Hey, who took my muffin?"

"Where's my biscuit?"

"My sandwiches are gone!"

Miss Hanson strode after them. "What's going on?"

I focused on my book, frantically writing. Four times four was...? Fifteen divided by–

"Miss," Sarah called, "Sean sneaked into the cloakroom during math time."

"Really?" Miss Hanson came over.

Sarah nodded. "While you were helping Amanda."

Sarah deserved every stupid spit-ball that we'd aimed at her – and more.

Miss Hanson fumed. Was that smoke coming out of her nostrils?

"OK, everyone," she called, "outside for morning tea."

"But mine's missing," whined Ginny.

"Get something else. Outside, now!"

Miss Hanson smiled. "Sean, why were you in the cloakroom?"

"I heard some rustling and went to see."

"What did you find?"

"Nothing. There was no one there," I said.

"Except you, Sean. You were there. Were you hungry?"

Should I tell her about Bob? Mum was always telling me to be honest. I doubted it would work this time, but maybe it was worth a try. "Miss, I'm not crazy, but a dragon stole snacks from the kids' lunchboxes."

"Sean, I don't think you're crazy."

"You don't, Miss Hanson?"

"No. I think you're lying," she said. "Did you take the other children's treats?"

I groaned and shook my head.

Miss Hanson stood. "Finish your math. At lunchtime you have a detention in the garden with Mr. Grinchov."

After bolting my lunch, I trudged behind the school hall to the garden, miles away from my friends. Mr Grinchov, the school caretaker, towered over me, grinning, the gaping holes in his mouth nearly big enough for a mouse to squeeze through – well, maybe a small one.

"Grab that shovel," he said. "Spread this sheep manure over that empty vegetable bed, then dig it in. Watch out for rats."

Rats? In this stinking dung? Surely he was joking?

Sweat trickled down my neck as I shoveled smelly sheep poo into the vegetable garden. The kids on the playground were yelling and having fun. No one came to see me. Everyone thought I was a thief.

"You're working well, Sean," said Mr. Grinchov. "I'm going to the staffroom for ten minutes. I want that finished by the time I'm back." Grinchov left to eat lunch.

"Where's that silly dragon?" I muttered, burying dung deep in the soil.

"Here!"

I jumped in fright. Bob appeared in the dung pile – two yellow eyes among the poo.

"Oh no, now you'll stink. You can't go back in my desk."

"You stink too," said Bob, "so no one will notice."

"You got me in trouble."

Bob leapt out of the dung, his scales changing to brilliant orange.

"Wow, you've grown!"

He ducked his head. "I'm sorry, that's why I had to eat." Bob looked around. "I can fix your pooey problem." Flames shot from his jaws, incinerating the dried sheep dung. In a moment, only ash was left – and a cloud of smelly smoke.

"No! Now, I'll get in more trouble." I ripped off my hoodie and waved it at the smoke, trying to disperse it.

Grinchov came running.

Bob leapt onto the grass, turning green – invisible in an instant.

"That's it young man!" yelled Grinchov. "It's illegal for twelve-year olds to smoke."

"But I didn't! The dragon did."

"Straight to the principal," he said.

Mr. Davies, the principal, didn't believe me either.

"But the dragon set the dung on fire."

"Some people call their cigarettes dragons, Sean." Mr. Davies shook his head. "But it's still illegal."

The police and Dad came to school and lectured me about how dangerous cigarettes were. I just nodded. No one was going to believe me.

They decided I should work in the school gardens every lunch hour for three weeks.

"It's all your fault, Bob." I sulked.

"I can help, Sean. Watch this!" Bob wrenched weeds out of the garden with his jaws, his talons flinging dirt.

"That's not enough." I shook my head. "I've got to get good at math. Hey, I know! You can help me with basic facts."

Every lunch hour for three weeks, Bob clung to my back like a rucksack, camouflaged blue like my hoodie, whispering times tables in my ear. I got good at math, Bob grew fat on rats, and no one suspected a thing.

One day after finishing early, I sat alone, tossing scraps from my lunchbox into the air. Bob leapt from the grass, snapping them up, turning from green to dazzling orange – and back to green again as he landed.

"Oh my!" a familiar voice gasped.

I spun. Bob ducked into the bushes, turning green again.

Miss Hanson had her hand over her mouth, her eyes wide. "A dragon! You *were* telling the truth!" She sunk down onto a bench, shaking. "Oh Sean, I've been the real dragon, getting mad at you for being honest."

Her? A dragon? Her hair was fiery. But had smoke really come out of her nostrils? Or had I only imagined it?

"Don't worry, Miss Hanson," I said. "Even though they get me into trouble, I quite like dragons!"

"I did too at your age," she said. "Especially math dragons."

I grinned. Did she mean me? Or Bob?

Golden Days

Chapter One – Bernie

My friends are playing at the park across the road – kicking a ball, riding the flying fox, and spinning on that awful round-about that used to make me dizzy. The brown-haired boy with the brace on his leg watches from the bench, sometimes waving to the others. I used to feel sorry for him when it was me playing.

Now, I want to be outside watching from the bench, like him, instead of stuck in my sick bed. My immune system, like an old-fashioned watch, is slowly winding down until it stops. Turning away from the window, I scratch my sore arms.

Mom bustles in. A white mask covers her mouth and nose. Just inside the door, she sanitizes her hands and pulls on latex gloves.

Sanitizer to stop infection coming in. Gloves to stop my skin getting worse. "Did you enjoy that book, Samantha?" Her voice quivers. She's afraid.

I don't blame her. I am too. "Sure," I say. The kids are playing Frisbee now, throwing the orange disk in wide arcs, laughing when they catch it. I touch the glass, wishing I could join in.

Mom reaches into her bag. "I bought you a new book." She puts on her brave smile. "Egypt yesterday. The Amazon today. This one should be fun."

I make another mark in my journal. That's 527 books in 165 days. I don't want more books. All I want is a hug, but she's afraid she'll give me another infection. I try to smile. "Thanks, Mom. Will you read with me?"

"Sure, honey, later. I'm going into town, now. Hannah is making dinner. Call her if you need anything." Her eyes slide to my arms. "Stop scratching. Please, sweetie." She bites her lip.

I place book 527 on my windowsill, and put my arms under the duvet where she can't see. "Have a nice time, Mom."

"You too, darling." Smiling apologetically, she peels the gloves off and tosses them in the bin by the door. She gives me a little wave and rushes out.

I get it. This is hard for Mom.

But what about me?

Sighing, I pick up the book and open the cover. Another adventure novel. Today I'll be stomping through the Amazon in search of an ancient talisman. Good old Mom. She knows I can't go out, so she brings the world to me.

Something taps on my window pane, *rat-a-tat-tat*, like a woodpecker. It makes me start.

Dropping the book, I stare at the boy outside the glass. It's him – the boy with the brace. I'd know his straight brown hair anywhere. His eyes are blue. Large. Serious. He knocks again. "Open it," he calls.

I unfasten the catch, pushing the window open. "Hi."

"Hello." He smiles, then his eyes take in my raw skin.

"It's okay, you can't catch it."

"It makes no difference, I'm sick already." He raises his eyebrows. "Are you going to die?"

I nod.

"Me too," he says, so quietly, I barely hear him. "Can I come in? I have something to show you." He opens a canvas satchel hanging from his shoulder. Inside, something golden glints.

"What is it?"

He winks. "Let me in and I'll show you."

He's my first real visitor in months. Mom's out and Hannah's busy. They'll never know. "There's a key under the purple flower pot by the mailbox."

He screws up his nose and grins. "I'll just climb in." He hoists his good leg over the window sill and drags his other leg up with his hands, then drops to the floor. Jammed between the wall and my bed, he's closer than anyone has been for ages.

I point to the small table by the door. "You'll need sanitizer and a mask and gloves."

He puts the mask on upside-down. The

gloves are too big and dangle like empty balloons from the ends of his fingers. Laughing, he blows at the mask, making it puff out like a bullfrog's throat. His eyes twinkle. He keeps puffing up the mask until I laugh too – although it makes me break into a coughing fit.

"Does that hurt?"

I nod, still coughing, and he pats my back, the first time anyone except Mom or the doctor has touched me in months. Tears prick my eyes.

He perches on the edge of my bed, reaches into his bag, and takes out a book. "I came to show you this."

Is that all? A book? My first visitor in ages, and he brings me another book. The smile melts from my face like ice cream dribbling off a cone. Book 528. "Oh. Thanks."

He places the book – a large golden one – in my hands. Our fingers bump, but he doesn't flinch, like Mom. The cover blurs. I blink back tears and sit up straight. "What's your name?"

"Bernie."

"I'm Samantha."

"Go on, open it."

"I'd rather talk. I've read enough lately."

He laughs. "I'm not asking you to read, just to open it." He touches the gold cover. It's embossed with *Golden Days* in old-fashioned writing. Twirling vines and berries encircle a dragon who's breathing fire at a knight. The paint's raised and peaky like the oil paintings our class saw in the city gallery last year, before I got sick.

Fairy tales? I'm about to snort in disgust, but Bernie looks so hopeful that I smile instead.

"Go on," he whispers. "Open it."

I trace the vines. The ridges of gold are warm, and hum beneath my fingers. I try to open the cover, but it won't budge. I try again. "I get it!" I say. "It's a trick book. It doesn't open, does it?"

Bernie places his gloved hand on the cover, and murmurs, "Open book, open book, let Samantha take a look."

The cover vibrates, then shakes and flips open. Pages flutter as if there's a storm in the room. They slow, and fall open at a majestic red dragon flying above a lush forest. Its scales gleam. Wisps of smoke trail from its nostrils, and its cheeky grin reveals large fangs. The clouds are so fluffy, I want to snuggle them. The trees look alive. Tracing my finger over the dragon' back, I *feel* its scales. Impossible. It's only a picture. I touch the dragon's nose. Is that smoke curling around my finger?

Bernie's eyes are bigger, bluer, than before.

I stare at him. "How could smoke – Ow!" I yank my finger off the book.

Bernie grins. "Watch out. Horatio likes to nip people when they're not looking!"

"Horatio?" He must mean the dragon.

A roar fills the room. Wind swirls around us. In a blast of light, my room and bed disappear. I'm sitting behind Bernie on the dragon, rocketing upwards through strands of cloud.

CHAPTER TWO – HORATIO

Bernie laughs, clinging to the dragon with his legs. His brace is gone and he's wearing old-fashioned brown clothes.

Instead of pajamas, I'm wearing a soft leather top, rough-spun trousers and boots. I breathe deeply, inhaling the scent of leather and fresh air – the first fresh air I've breathed in months. My lungs feel strong. I fill them without coughing. Without pain. My arms aren't sore and itchy. I pull my sleeves back. My skin is healed! I can't help grinning.

The dragon roars and a spurt of green flame shoots from its maw, leaving smoky residue in the air. I laugh, wrinkling my nose as we fly through the wisps of green-tinged smoke.

Green flame and smoke? This place is weird. Am I dreaming? Trapped in a book? Or in another world?

We soar into the sky, towards a snow-tipped mountain. A warm glow envelopes me, despite the icy cliff-face looming in front of us. The pine trees in the forest below are like toothpicks. Beneath us, the dragon rumbles, its sides vibrating against our legs. Bernie whoops!

"This is great," I call, my words drifting on the breeze.

"I know," he cries. "I can use both of my legs again!" He kicks them like a toddler in a paddling pool.

A tiny high-pitched voice drifts on the breeze. "Help! Help me."

The dragon swoops downwards, making my stomach clench. Horatio lands on a snow-covered ledge halfway up the mountain. We slide off his back into the snow and bump against the cliff-face rising vertically above us. A rope ladder, encrusted with ice, hangs against the mountainside.

A voice rumbles through my mind. *"Samantha and Bernie, I'm too big to help."* It's the dragon, Horatio, speaking in our heads. Wow, he's using telepathy. That's awesome. *"Someone needs to be rescued. Go quickly, but be careful. Call me if you need me."* His legs bunching and huge wings rustling, Horatio leaps off the ledge.

"We have to help." Bernie tugs me to the ladder. The rungs stretch into grey swirling mist.

"Help me!" The cry is faint, but it's definitely coming from the top of the rope ladder. I blow on my hands, my breath gusting in silver clouds, then start to climb. The cold rope bites into my fingers.

"You can do it, Samantha." Bernie is right behind me.

The cries spur us on. "Help, get me out of here. Please!"

The rope sways as we shift our weight from rung to rung, but soon we're in rhythm, moving in time to counterbalance each other. The icy rock face scrapes our knuckles. The voice sounds weaker, tired.

Soon it stops.

I can't see how far there is to go. Wisps of cloud obscure my view. We keep climbing, hand over hand, foot over foot, slowly getting higher. Grey feathery fingers brush across my face, leaving damp trails on my cheeks.

"Bernie, I can hardly feel my hands, and my feet are Popsicles."

"M–me t–too," he replies with chattering teeth. "C–can you s–see the t–top?"

"Not yet." Doubt gnaws inside me. My foot slips on a rung, yanking my shoulder sockets.

"Whoa," Bernie calls, "hang on." He guides my boot back onto the rope.

Horatio rumbles inside my head. *"You can do this. Keep going."* I turn at the sound of his voice, but can't see a dragon – only clouds.

The ladder ends abruptly. Bernie and I clamber onto a rocky windswept shelf. The mouth of a dark cave yawns in the rock. "There's nowhere else to go," Bernie says. "Come on."

The cave narrows and becomes a winding tunnel through the mountain. "What's that glimmering around the corner?" I tug Bernie forward.

Beyond the bend, torches flicker with green flame. "More green flames," Bernie says, "just like Horatio's fire."

The tunnel winds on, getting warmer the further we walk. "This doesn't make sense," I say. "We're in a mountain. It should be freezing."

We round a corner. And stop.

"What's making that light?" Bernie stares upwards to solve the mystery.

"Those beetles, somehow. Look…"

Shafts of light stream from strange glowing beetles on the roof of a high cavern, bathing a cottage at the edge of a grassy glade in a yellow glow. Rabbits frolic among daffodils and bluebells, and fawns nibble grass. Birds nest in fir trees, tweeting a beautiful melody.

"Wow." Bernie's face is radiant with wonder. He can hear it too.

The music draws us in, our feet moving before we can think.

The cottage's brown walls are painted with designs in pastel pink, yellow and blue. The roof looks as if it's made of white frosting. A delicious scent wafts on the breeze.

"What's that awesome smell?" Bernie asks.

"It reminds me of Christmas." My mouth waters. I inhale deeply. "Nutmeg, cinnamon and ginger."

"Gingerbread!" he says, "The house is made of gingerbread!" His stomach rumbles.

Bernie rushes forward and breaks off a piece of gingerbread windowsill, shoveling it in his mouth.

A gingerbread house? Like Hansel and Gretel! "No, Bernie! Stop! Don't swallow it!"

The same high voice calls, "It's a trap. The gingerbread is poisonous."

I gaze at Bernie in horror, and then snatch the gingerbread out of his hand. "Bernie, it's poisonous. Didn't you hear the voice?"

He spits the gingerbread out and hurls the rest into the trees. "Luckily, I didn't swallow any."

"Look!" I whisper. "They're not really rabbits." The rabbits' ears shrink then disappear. Their soft fur shrivels away revealing huge rats with sharp teeth. "And those fawns…" The fawns flicker, looking like hyenas. The birds' melody dies, turning into rasping croaks from the mouths of scrawny crows.

"Let me out, please." The voice is coming from a cage hanging on the side of the cottage, a cage so small we hadn't noticed it. We approach and look inside.

A tiny winged girl, smaller than my hand, is lying on her side, clutching her stomach. Her skin shimmers with golden flecks and her hair is dark. Her blue eyes remind me of Bernie's. "It's a fairy," I murmur.

"Her name is Aurora," says Bernie. "I met her on my first adventure in *Golden Days*."

"Horatio said you'd rescue me." Aurora's eyes light up as if we're a Christmas gift, but then she winces and presses her hands to her stomach. "I was hungry. I ate poisoned gingerbread and a witch caught me. She wants my magic, and she's going to drain my blood to get it."

"That's awful." I grab the door to the cage.

"Careful," cries the fairy, too late. The bars are covered in slime that stings my fingers – making them throb. "It's witch sting," the fairy whimpers. "That's why no one can rescue me."

She clutches her stomach tighter. The gold flecks on her skin grow dim. "The poison... I'm dying."

I wipe my stinging hand on the grass. It wilts where I touch it. "We have to get her out!" I meet Bernie's eyes.

"Eating a dragon's scale will cure me," Aurora whispers.

"Dragon's scale?" asks Bernie. "Horatio can give you one."

"But I still have to get free." The fairy's eyes grow round with fear as cackling comes from the cottage. "Quick. Hide! The witch is coming."

We rush into the trees, hiding behind the trunk of a large fir.

The cottage door flies open and a beautiful woman with curly red hair stomps out. "Ha, ha," she cries. "Soon my poison will dissolve your bones, and I'll drink them with your fairy blood." Her voice is scratchy and hoarse, but her face is young.

Stomping around the cottage, she glares at the fairy. "My spell is fading. Soon my beauty will disappear. I need more fairy bones and blood." Her face flickers, suddenly warty and wrinkled with grey hair, then she looks young again, her red hair glinting in the unnatural glow around the cottage. "Hurry up and die," she shouts, "so I can mix your bones and blood into my beauty smoothie."

The witch pulls a silver scarf from her pocket and wraps it around her hands. She opens the cage and picks up the fairy, squeezing her. "Not ready yet! Your bones are still too firm!" She tosses the fairy against the bars. "But soon you'll be ready! And I'll be beautiful forever!" The witch stalks back into the cottage, cackling.

I dash forward and snatch the scarf as it flutters to the ground, wrapping it around my hands. My fingers buzz with strange energy as I yank the cage door open, but they don't sting. Gently, Bernie lifts Aurora from the cage and passes her to me.

She's tiny, limp in my hands, but still warm. The gold on her skin has faded to pale freckles. I wrap the scarf around her and tuck her inside my leather shirt, against my chest. Bernie and I dash towards the tunnel.

Behind us, the cottage door bangs open. "Aagh!" the witch screams. "Fairy robbers!" Her shoes clatter on the stone as she chases us.

The witch's mad cackle bounces off the

tunnel walls, echoing like a hundred fighting cats. We race. My heart thumps. Bernie's breath comes in gasps. Our feet pound on stone. I cradle my hand against my shirt to protect the fairy. A flash of yellow light shoots down the tunnel. We swerve, then spurt ahead.

More light flashes. Pain sears my arm.

Bernie bursts onto the ledge, dragging me with him, the witch close behind.

"Horatio," he yells.

With a whoosh of wings, Horatio swoops, plucking us up in his large talons, and races high into the blue sky. On the ledge below, the witch jumps up and down, shrieking and flinging fire bolts after us.

"She's having a tantrum – with fireworks!" Bernie laughs, then becomes serious. "Are you okay?"

"My arm's sore, but Aurora's dying. She needs a dragon's scale."

"Hold on tight," calls Horatio. He dives down the mountainside towards the forest. Trees loom as we approach. The dragon circles a grassy clearing, then drops us gently

to the ground and lands nearby.

Bernie's eyes are worried.

I reach into my leather top and take Aurora out, cradling her in my fingers. "I'm not sure if we're too late…"

"Be my guest." Horatio extends a leg. Bernie plucks a translucent red scale from Horatio's limb. The light catches the scale, making it sparkle. Bernie presses it against the fairy's lips.

Her eyes flutter. She opens them, and takes the scale in her tiny fingers. She's so small it looks like she's nibbling on a dinner plate as she takes delicate bites of dragon armor.

"Thank you," she whispers.

With each bite, Aurora's skin color changes. Her pale freckles glimmer, then glow, then become shiny gold flecks again. She eats until her skin is golden and her eyes spark blue. "Thank you Horatio," she says, "that was delicious – even better than fairy cakes."

"You're welcome," he rumbles.

"Thank you for rescuing me, Samantha and Bernie," Aurora says. "You've proven yourself worthy to visit our kingdom whenever you wish. My book, *Golden Days*, will always be open for you."

My cheeks grow warm.

Bernie blushes too. "It was nothing," he says.

CHAPTER THREE – KNIGHTS

In a flash of light, Bernie and I are sitting on my bed again with *Golden Days* in our hands. The page is open at an illustration of a blue-eyed, golden-skinned fairy, perched on a dragon's nose.

Bernie closes the book and glances outside. "It's getting late," he says, packing the book into his satchel. "I'll see you again tomorrow."

I grin. "Cool. Don't forget *Golden Days*."

He clambers out the window and I wave goodbye. Suddenly my sickbed doesn't seem like such a prison.

The next day, I can hardly concentrate on the adventure books Mom brings me. I keep glancing out the window, waiting for the kids to arrive at the park. Bernie only sits on the bench for a few minutes before limping across the road to my place.

Hoisting his leg through the window, he sits on my bed. "Want to read again?" he asks, blue eyes twinkling.

"I'd love to."

He passes me a book from my shelf.

"Hey!"

Laughing, he gives me *Golden Days*. As soon as I touch the cover, the pages fly open. Light flashes. A roar fills my ears and wind sweeps me and Bernie away.

We land in the courtyard of a castle, wearing full body armor and helmets. Horses stamp and snort. People rush to and fro, grabbing weapons and harnessing the horses. Far off, a bell is ringing.

"Hey, you young knights!" a large man in a dirty canvas apron bellows at us. "Take these two horses, and get your weapons."

"Uh, thank you, sir." Bernie nods and takes the reins, passing one set to me.

We lead the horses to a stand of weapons – crossbows, longbows, spears and swords.

"What'll it be?" asks a man. He has so many gaps in his mouth, I can count his teeth on three fingers.

"Spears," I say quickly, keeping my voice deep so he thinks I'm a boy. I have no idea how to use bows and arrows, and the thought of using a sword makes my knees shake. At least a spear means we won't get too close – I hope.

"And shields," says Bernie, getting one for each of us.

A tall knight – with shoulders as broad farm gate, and a needle-shaped nose guard on his helmet – bellows at everyone to mount their horses.

"How do we mount horses?" I mutter to Bernie. "I can hardly move in this armor."

This is obviously a common problem. All over the courtyard, servants are helping knights onto their horses. Bernie hoists me onto my horse, then someone gives him a leg up. I've been on a horse once or twice before, but this feels stiff and uncomfortable, like I'm going to fall off any moment.

Needle-nose gives the command, "Ride out."

"Yes, Sir Prance-a-lot," the armored men call.

The throng of knights presses towards the courtyard gates and we're swept along, armor clanking and hooves pounding the cobbles.

"Where are we going?" Bernie asks a little

knight on a roan horse.

The little knight rolls his eyes, as if Bernie is dumb. "Can't you hear the bell? King George's nets have trapped the dragon, so we're off to slay it."

Bernie's face pales.

My heart sinks. So far, I've only met one dragon in *Golden Days*. "What's the dragon done?" I ask.

"Nothing, so far," says the knight.

"Then why's the king killing it?" asks Bernie.

The little knight rolls his eyes again and trots off.

"Move out," calls Sir Prance-a-lot.

Three abreast, we're jostled along into the woods and through a trail, until we come to a meadow. I recognize this place. We healed Aurora here. On the far side of the clearing, strung from the trees, is a giant net. Inside, a magnificent red dragon is writhing, shooting flame at two knights nearby.

A red dragon. Bernie and I glance at each other. Is it Horatio?

Sir Prance-a-lot barks at the knights. "The

one who slays this beast will gain favor with the king and have the princess's hand in marriage. Any volunteers?"

The dragon roars. The ground quivers. It could be Horatio. He's red and about the same size. The beast opens his jaws and blasts fire halfway across the clearing, setting the grass alight. Knights scramble to stamp it out. The dragon twists and thrashes. The boughs holding the net groan under his weight.

The knights around us stare at the ground. "Rather b-big, isn't it?" says one.

"A bit scary," agrees another.

Clanking reaches my ears. The little knight who rolled his eyes at Bernie is trembling so hard his armor's rattling.

Sir Prance-a-lot's horse dances nervously on the spot. He tugs its reins, calling, "So, who will volunteer?"

Bernie urges his horse forward. "I volunteer."

"You?!" Sir Prance-a-lot sneers. "A scrawny boy?" He passes his sword to Bernie, gesturing at Bernie's spear. "You'll need more than that toothpick to kill this beast."

Bernie tosses the sword to the ground. His voice rings across the clearing. "I didn't say I would slay the dragon, and I don't need the princess's hand in marriage, but I volunteer. I'll *tame* the dragon."

"Tame a dragon? Preposterous! Ridiculous," Sir Prance-a-lot scoffs, trying to control his horse. He hoots with laughter. The other knights whoop and snigger.

I urge my horse forward to stand by Bernie's. "I'll help," I say in my best deepest voice. "We're dragon tamers. Sam and Bernie, at your service."

If it's not Horatio, we're dragon's toast.

Sir Prance-a-lot waves the group to silence. "So, two cheeky boys volunteer, putting the king's best knights to shame. I'll not have that." I cringe, imagining what he'd say if he realizes I'm a girl. He bellows, "The king has ordered this dragon to be slain, not tamed! Seize them. Drag them off to the dungeons." He swats at a winged insect zipping around his face. "Now!"

Knights rush forward, seizing Bernie and I by the arms, dragging us off our horses.

The insect lands on Sir Prance-a-lot's hair. Only it's not an insect – it's a tiny gold fairy with blue eyes. Bernie gasps. He's seen Aurora too. She sprinkles fairy dust over Sir Prance-a-lot's head.

Sir Prance-a-lot's face breaks into a huge smile. "What a great idea: taming the dragon. Unhand those delightful children and let them tame that ferocious beast." He gestures us forward, across the meadow.

A ripple of concern flows through the knights.

"They can't believe we're approaching such a wild beast on foot," says Bernie.

"Those silly knights. We know Horatio is friendly." I try not to giggle.

"If it's Horatio," says Bernie.

"And if he recognizes us in all this armor."

Bernie's hands shake. "I have an idea. Let's hope it works." As we approach the net, he sings loudly,

Horatio, Horatio
Over hill and forest you go
Horatio, Horatio
Your wings are vast and fire you blow

Horatio, Horatio
Sam and Bernie are here, you know
So Horatio, Horatio
Be friendly when we let you go.

The mighty red dragon stops thrashing. It *is* Horatio! He tilts his head to listen to Bernie's song. Sir Prance-a-lot and the knights gape.

I cut the net with my spear tip. "Escape, Horatio, escape!"

But Horatio nudges my stomach and purrs like an oversized kitten. I scratch his nose. His voice rumbles through my mind, and I know Bernie hears it too. *"I'm so glad to see you both. Let's show them how you can tame me."*

The great dragon rolls onto his back and shows his stomach. Scaly limbs – powerful enough to kill a full-grown man – kick the air. Bernie leans in and pats Horatio's belly.

The knights gasp.

"He's only a boy and so brave," a knight murmurs.

"Impossible," murmurs another.

I clap and twirl my hands in a rolling motion. Horatio obliges, flipping over to sit.

Bernie climbs on Horatio's back and I clamber up behind him. We pump our arms high in the air. Bernie cries out, "The dragon is tamed."

One of the knights starts clapping. "It worked," he yells. They all join in.

A flicker of fire bursts from Horatio's jaws and we shoot up, leaving the knights in the forest.

"Thank you," says Horatio. *"Not only have you saved Aurora, but now you've saved me. If you ever choose to, you can stay in Golden Days forever."*

In a flash of light, Bernie and I are back, sitting in my room.

CHAPTER FOUR – GOLDEN DAYS

Bernie shuts the book and tucks it in his satchel. "I'd better get home." He slips out the window.

"Come again tomorrow," I call.

He grins and waves.

Bernie doesn't only come tomorrow, he comes every day, bringing *Golden Days* so we can have adventures. Sometimes, we have quiet picnics in the forest or at a river's edge. Other times, Horatio takes us to battle monsters, help centaurs trapped in the forest, or save a princess from wicked robbers. Aurora asks us to help stop the gingerbread witch from capturing children, to tame goblins, and to help fairies learn to read.

Bernie visits me for weeks. I'm not sure if it's my imagination, but it seems to be taking him longer to climb in my window.

Soon he's definitely walking slower. He has to rest on the sill while climbing inside.

"Are you okay?"

Bernie pants for a moment, then grins. "Just tired today," he replies, and opens

*Golden Day*s.

One day, he doesn't come. I sit in bed, staring out the window until night falls. When Mom comes to say goodnight, I ask her to leave the light on. It glares all night, waiting for Bernie. I fall asleep as dawn arrives, and wake in the afternoon to children's laughter in the park.

Bernie's not on the bench. He hasn't been for ages. He's been coming straight to visit me. I watch and wait for another night. Perhaps Bernie is taking a break…

And another night.

Mom hovers, plucking at my blankets. "Darling, are you alright? You seem a little down, lately."

I refuse to speak. I don't know if I'm alright. I don't know what's happening to Bernie.

Days pass. The doctor comes and goes.

Two weeks after Bernie's last visit, Mom enters my room holding a package wrapped in brown paper. I stare out the window. In the park, autumn leaves fall from the trees. Wind swirls them in eddies across the dying grass.

Mom comes over to my bed. Giving me the parcel, she smiles. "This was in the mailbox."

The package is heavy in my hands. I swallow. It's book-shaped. The same size as *Golden Days*. The writing on the front is a child's. *For Samantha in the blue house across from the park*. Throat tight, I blink. Bernie really is gone. He's left me his book.

Hot tears slide down my face, their salty tang dribbling over my lips. *Bernie is gone*.

Dismay ripples across Mom's face. "I thought this would make you happy. I didn't know–" She tries to snatch the package from me.

"No!" I scream, clutching it to my chest. "No! Go away!"

Mom rushes out. I hear her broken voice in the living room, and Hannah comforting her. I burrow under my blankets, Bernie's parcel against me, and cry myself to sleep.

Every day I sit, staring out the window, his package on my lap. The trees are bare, their naked boughs stretching against the sky. Mom brings me books. They sit in random stacks on my bedside table, the window sill, the floor. Unread.

Outside, snow falls. The thermostat in my room says it's warm, but my insides are icy. Days crawl slower than a snail up a sunflower stem.

Nights are worse. I dream of Bernie, laughing as we fly on Horatio over the forest. And I miss him even more when I wake.

One evening, I overhear the doctor's concerned mumble from the hall. "She's getting weaker. I'm sorry, it won't be long now."

Mom's voice shakes, but I can't make out her quiet reply. I drift to sleep.

Loud humming wakes me. It's the package. Sitting up, I trace Bernie's writing with my finger.

Carefully removing the tape, I peel back the brown paper, smoothing the wrinkles from it. This is from him. It's precious. I tuck the paper under my pillow.

I won't visit *Golden Days*. Not without Bernie.

I let my fingers trail over the embossed patterns on the golden cover. There, among the vines and leaves, I glimpse a tiny fairy. Aurora. I've never noticed her there before. The book's humming grows louder, the vibration running through my fingers and up my arm.

Aurora flits off the cover and tugs my finger. High-pitched fairy song rings in my ears. In a flash of light, I'm in the grassy clearing, the *Golden Days'* forests around me. The scent of wildflowers drifts on the air.

A roar makes the air tremble. Horatio swoops down to land.

Bernie leaps from his back and hugs me. He's strong. Stronger than ever. He's not dead at all. "Samantha, you're here," he says. "You're finally here. I've been waiting for ages."

Horatio's voice rumbles, *"Samantha, I'm pleased you're back."*

"Bernie, I thought you were… I mean, I didn't know…"

Bernie gazes at me. "Samantha, I can't go back. My time on earth is over." He smiles. "But you can stay. Please stay in *Golden Days*, so all of our days can be golden."

Aurora whizzes around his head, then comes to land on my hand. Her fairy voice comes to me clearly. "Samantha, you must make a choice."

"What do you mean?"

"You have a few more days on earth, at the most," Aurora says, "but you can choose to live on, if you stay here."

"I can't do that to my Mom."

Bernie nods, and hugs me once more. "I understand."

Then he turns and clambers onto Horatio's back. They soar into the air. Bernie waves goodbye.

"See you soon, Samantha," Horatio rumbles.

But they won't. They won't see me soon. I'm going home. I wave. Horatio flips his tail.

Aurora takes my hand. In a flash of light and whirl of fairy song, I'm home in bed again. *Golden Days* rests in my lap. I study the cover. Aurora is no longer hiding between the vines. But, there, behind the dragon's ear is what looks like a tiny golden insect. I know better.

In the forest behind the dragon, I spy a boy with straight brown hair. I'd know that hair anywhere.

I smile, even though the pain in my chest makes it hard to breathe.

Mom walks into my room. "Samantha, you look radiant."

I keep smiling. "Mom, I know I'm dying."

Mom gasps.

"It's okay," I say. "I love you. I'm still reading this book, but when I'm gone, I want you to have it." I show her *Golden Days*.

She gazes at the cover. "It's beautiful," she says. "I'm sorry you got sick."

"I'm not, Mom. I'm glad. Some of my best days have been since I got ill." I gaze at her. "And believe me, I have many more good days ahead of me."

I can tell from her trembling lip that she doesn't believe me. That she'll miss me. That she wishes things could be the way they were before I got ill.

"Promise me you'll read *Golden Days*."

"I will."

From the look in her eyes, I believe her.

After Mom has left, I scribble a note for her.

Mom,
You'll love this book.
I know you'll see me in these stories.
Love, Samantha xxx

I open *Golden Days*. Brilliant light streams from the pages. A roar fills my ears and I'm whisked into the sky, landing on Horatio behind Bernie.

"Yahoo," Bernie yells. I cling to his back.

Horatio roars. We swoop over the forest. Aurora peeks out from Horatio's ear.

"Welcome home," she says.

Bernie's laughter rings over the forest. Now all our days *will* be golden.

EPILOGUE – GOLDEN DAYS

I'm Samantha's mother, Charlotte Jenkins.

Samantha has been gone for years. Whenever I want to see her, I open the cover of *Golden Days* and visit. In her world, I'm always young. No stiff fingers and old aching bones.

My ringtone jangles.

Sighing, I place the large gold book on the table beside my rocking chair and pick up my phone.

"Hello?"

"Ms Jenkins?" a warm voice asks. "This is Henrietta Murray, charge nurse from the children's ward at Middleton Hospital. I was told you'd volunteered to be one of our storytellers."

"That's right. I called yesterday, but they told me they already had enough people."

"Unfortunately, one of our volunteers has fallen seriously ill, and I don't want to disappoint the children. Could you start this afternoon?"

"I'd be delighted." I smile, touching *Golden*

Days' cover. "I have the perfect book to share with them. It was my daughter's favorite."

Rumbled

I tiptoed down the staircase, guided by the glow of my wand, and peered around the door.

There it was, under the Christmas tree. A square box, wrapped in luxurious red velvet, perforated with air holes and tied with a golden bow. From it, hung Dad's annoying label: *For Seamus* or *Finneas*. Seamus and I both needed that present to enter the Junior Wizard and Mascot Race at Fogsnort's Wizard Academy on Christmas Day. But only one of us would get the magical animal inside.

I glanced behind me. The coast was clear.

Earlier that evening, Dad had brought the present home. "They were nearly sold out," he'd said, shaking his head. "There was only one mascot left, boys. Only one. You'll have to fight it out tomorrow morning."

"I'm eldest. It's mine," Seamus had hissed

as Dad left the room. He'd jabbed his fingers into my ribs, grabbed my skin and twisted, leaving bruises. "I'm going in that race, or I'll turn you into a warty toad. Loser."

Seamus would beat me. He always did.

During my last wizard trial, he'd hexed my potion so it splashed in Master Fogsnort's face, making him break out in nasty green boils. No one believed Seamus had been responsible.

A month ago, he beat me up, and told Mum and Dad my bruises were from crashing my broom on the way home. And only last week, he'd cast a stinkus spell on me. The stench of rotten eggs was so strong, no one would sit next to me all day.

I had to have that mascot.

We weren't allowed to unwrap Christmas presents until seven – Mum and Dad were super strict on that. But if I could hide the box from Seamus, then I could open it first. Gingerly carrying the velvet-wrapped box out of the living room, I padded across the cool kitchen tiles.

The box rumbled, making my arm hairs

stand on end. Toeing the pantry door open, I placed the shaking box on a shelf between a freshly-dusted plum cake and a meat pie.

My mouth watered.

I broke off some pie crust. A large chunk of meat and gravy came with it. Worried Mum might notice, I gobbled it up, grabbed my wand out of my pocket, and cast a glamour over the pie to make it look whole.

From inside the box came scratching and a vicious snarl. It swayed on the shelf, knocking the plum cake. I recoiled. What sort of wizarding mascot had Dad chosen? Not an owl. A gryphon? A phoenix? Perhaps something nastier.

Yowling came from the box. The screech of tearing fabric rent the air, and a curved claw poked through the velvet. Within seconds, the wrapping was a red flurry of slashed velvet.

Footfalls thumped down the stairs.

"Finneas, you cheat," bellowed Seamus. "That's unfair!"

As if *he'd* ever played fair!

The dispersing cloud of shredded velvet

revealed a tiny dragonet atop a jar of gherkins – eyes green and whirling, fangs bared, and talons out. The purple patch on her throat showed she was female.

A dragonet? My heart hammered. A dragonet!

"Come here," I crooned, "come on, girl."

The dragonet leapt onto my arm, licking my hand. Dragons. What had Master Fogsnort taught us? How could I imprint with a dragon?

Too late. The kitchen door crashed open. Seamus' ugly mug grimaced with rage.

His eyes lit up as he spied the dragonet. "It's mine!" Seamus bellowed, "I'll feed it."

Feed her? Yes, that was it! Dragons bonded with the first to feed them.

Seamus pushed past me and dashed to the fridge, then ran back, thrusting bloody strips of beef under the dragonet's nose. She snaffled the meat and let out an appreciative rumble.

He'd won again. He'd fed her first. It had all been for nothing.

"It's mine!" yelled Seamus, snatching for

the dragon.

Her claws dug into my arm. She flapped her wings, bared her fangs, and shot a jet of flame at Seamus, scorching his face.

"Aaagh!" Seamus ran from the room, his face in his hands. "Daaaad!"

Upstairs, my parents' door banged open.

The dragonet cocked her head at me. She leapt up on my shoulder and curled her tail around my neck, nuzzling into me, her body thrumming warmly against my skin.

Of course! She'd licked the gravy off my fingers. Seamus hadn't fed her first! I had!

Dad marched into the kitchen. He looked over at me, the dragonet and the shredded velvet – and raised his eyebrows.

Seamus trailed behind him, moaning, "I fed it first, Dad. It's mine. He stole it!"

"No, Seamus," said Dad firmly. "Can't you see the dragon escaped? Finneas didn't steal *her*. Although he will have to take down the Christmas tree himself this year, for getting up early."

Seamus scowled. "But Dad–"

"And you'll have to help him," Dad

scolded. "You're up early too." He smiled at me. "Congratulations are in order, Finneas. She's imprinted well."

She was mine. We would be racing together at Fogsnort's.

"Merry Christmas," I murmured to my new friend. "And a happier New Year!"

(*Rumbled* was published in *Twisty Christmas Tales* and *The Best of Twisty Christmas Tales*, Phantom Feather Press, 2013, 2014)

Preview: Dragons Realm

A You Say Which Way Adventure

Next generation storytelling where YOU say
which way the story goes.
http://bit.ly/1Mjcad1

DRAGONS REALM

Escaping the school bullies, you stumble into a world of dragons and magic. A voice that only you hear calls out for help. Will you answer? Who should you trust? Are the bullies behind you?

Luckily you packed a good picnic lunch for your adventure in Dragons' Realm.

What Amazon Reviewers are saying about *Dragons Realm*:

"Whatever path through Dragons Realm you choose, you're in for a rollicking fun-filled adventure. With dragons."

"My 7 year old son loved it. He was jumping around the room in excitement and took all the choices very seriously indeed."

"Cleverly conceived and well written, this is a gem of a novel."

A Bad Start

"Hey, Fart-face!"

Uh oh. The Thompson twins are lounging against a fence as you leave the corner store – Bart, Becks, and Bax. They're actually the Thomson triplets, but they're not so good at counting, so they call themselves twins. Nobody has dared tell them different.

They stare at you. Bart, big as an ox. Becks, smaller but meaner. And Bax, the muscle. As if they need it.

Bart grins like an actor in a toothpaste commercial. "What have you got?" He swaggers towards you.

Becks sneers, stepping out with Bax close behind. "Come on, squirt, hand it over," she calls, her meaty hands bunching into fists.

Your backpack is heavy with goodies. Ten chocolate bars and two cans of tuna fish for five bucks – how could you resist? And now you could lose it all.

The twins form a human wall, blocking the sidewalk. There's no way around them.

Seriously? All this fuss over chocolate? Not again! They've been bullying you and your friends for way too long. There's still time to outsmart them before the bus leaves for the school picnic.

A girl walks between you and the twins. You make your move, sprinting off towards the park next to school. Your backpack is heavy, but you've gained a head start on those numb skulls.

Becks roars.

"Charge," yells Bax,

"Get the snot-head," Bart bellows. Their feet pound behind you as you make it around the corner through the park gate. Now to find a hiding place.

On your right is a thick grove of trees. They'll never find you in there, not without missing the bus to the picnic.

To your left is a sports field. Behind the bleachers, there's a hole in the fence. If you can make it through that hole, you're safe. They're much too big to follow.

Their pounding footsteps are getting closer. They'll be around the corner soon.

It is time to make a decision. Do you:

Race across the park to the hole in the fence?

Or

Hide from the Thompson twins in the trees?

Read more on Amazon:

http://bit.ly/1Mjcad1

Preview: Attack on Dragons Realm

amazon.com/Eileen-Mueller/e/B00HBHSIO0

ATTACK ON DRAGONS REALM

Drums pound the danger signal. Tharuks are attacking Dragons Realm. How can three unlikely heroes turn the tide of battle?

Jerrick, a dragon rider, is scared of flying. Benno is a warrior who faints when he thinks of blood, and Reina is a wizard whose magic backfires.

But monsters are coming and they must now fight to save their families.

"Thrilling and suspenseful."

–Amazon Reviewer

DRUMBEATS

Jerrick started awake. Drums were pounding. The cabin was pulsing, like a giant's heartbeat. He yanked his goatskin jerkin over his nightshirt. In a sliver of moonlight, Pa stumbled out of bed. Fumbling for his trousers and boots, Jerrick tugged them on. His heart thumped in time to the drums. *Danger.*

Susi, just a littling, whimpered. Ma hushed her, stroking her hair.

"Here." Pa thrust a sword into Jerrick's hand and picked up a sword and club for himself.

Jerrick gulped. His sword was suddenly heavy, awkward in his grip. For years he'd practiced fighting with Benno and Reina, although they'd never been in battle yet. But that was about to change.

He kissed Ma's cheek and ruffled Susi's hair, then he snatched up his bow and quiver, and ran out the door after Pa.

Drumbeats rolled off the thatched roofs of

Horseshoe Bend, throbbing though him. A tide of bodies swept them through narrow alleys between cottages, towards the settlement square. Like a hunting dog, Pa was fully alert, body tense.

In the thick of the crowd, someone squeezed Jerrick's arm. Gripping his sword, he spun. It was Benno. "Oh, it's you." Jerrick's breath whooshed out in relief. "What's going on?"

"Attack," Benno said. "Pa's been fighting half the night and just came back, wounded."

"Is he alright?"

Benno's face was pale. "The healer is with him. He'll live, but tharuks slashed him up bad."

His Pa's injuries must've been awful if Benno was pale – he was tough. "Tharuks?" asked Jerrick. "What are they?"

"Monsters." Benno grimaced. "They came to Dragons' Realm through a world gate."

"Monsters? From another world? You're joking!" But the look on Benno's face told Jerrick he wasn't. His neck hairs prickled. Benno's Pa was Horseshoe Bend's woodcutter – built like a draft horse and twice as strong. If he was wounded, these monsters must be bad.

Breaking out from between the cottages, they came to the square in the centre of the Horseshoe Bend. Pa pulled Jerrick and Benno to the front of the crowd. In the fire pit, a bonfire blazed, flames licking skywards. Sweat-beaded drummers beat their tattoo, *danger, danger, danger.*

"Look, there's Reina," Benno yelled over the drums.

Where? In the dancing shadows from the flickering fire, Jerrick couldn't see her – until she waved. He motioned her over.

Reina skirted around the sea of folk.

The whole settlement was here – all but the littlings and their mothers. The drums were exhilarating, goading Jerrick to action – making him want to run, to fight, to charge an unseen enemy like a madman.

Reina reached them. "Hey, Jerrick, Benno. At last we get to fight!" She grinned, despite the danger.

"Benno's Pa has been hurt," Jerrick blurted

out.

"He fought with Giant John," said Benno, puffing up his chest. "Killed a tharuk, too."

"Monsters...." Reina shook her head. "Crazy stuff! But our wizards will stop them."

"Come on, Reina." Jerrick rolled his eyes. "We all know dragons are stronger."

Before Reina could reply, Gowp, the settlement leader and arbitrator, held up his hand. The drumbeats stopped. In the sudden hush, the bonfire crackled. The air hummed with fear and anticipation.

A whoosh came from behind them. Jerrick's hair ruffled. Folk whirled. And gasped. Against the dark night sky, a majestic bronze dragon glimmered in the firelight. The dragon circled down, folk scrambling out of its way. The bronze beauty settled low to the ground. Three people slid off its back.

Clad in rider's breeches and jerkin, with a bow and quiver of arrows across his back, a dragon rider approached Gowp. Behind the rider was Master Giddi, head of the Wizard Council with bristly dark hair, his face smeared with soot and his eyes wild. At the rear was Giant John, head of Horseshoe Bend's warriors – as broad as two men, and more than two heads above the crowd.

Murmurs rippled through the square as the three men spoke with Gowp, their faces grim. Gowp grimaced, shaking his head.

"Hey," said Benno, "that's tharuk blood." He pointed at black liquid glinting on Giant John's jerkin. "My Pa was covered in that stuff."

"Master Giddi is awesome," Reina whispered, staring at him like a puppy at the leader of a pack. "Look at his face. He's been using wizard fire."

Jerrick nudged Benno, pointing to the dragon rider with dark curly hair. "That rider only looks about eighteen, just a few years older than us. That could be me, some day."

"Five," Benno said, "that's five years older, Jerrick."

"Yeah, but look at that dragon…" Jerrick stared. The flickering firelight made the dragon's scales shimmer. "A bronze. She's beautiful."

As if aware of his gaze, the dragon turned.

Its nostrils flared and it snorted.

"Watch out, Jerrick." Reina snorted, almost sounding like the dragon, but not quite. "You're drooling."

Despite her humor, Jerrick's belly was tight with tension.

Holding up his hand, Gowp turned. A hush fell over the square.

"We've been attacked," Gowp announced. "Tonight tharuks – strange new monsters who have invaded Dragons' Realm – sneaked up on Horseshoe Bend. But Hans, Master Giddi, Giant John and some of our best warriors defeated their scouting party." He gestured towards the dragon rider. "Hans has a message from Zaarusha, the Dragon Queen."

Wow, a direct message from the ruling dragon. Jerrick had never seen her, but they said Zaarusha was so beautiful her scales rippled with every color of the rainbow.

"Greetings from Dragons' Hold," said Hans. "Tharuks want our Realm. They're terrorizing our folk. Our dragons can't be everywhere, so settlements must prepare their own fighting forces."

Grumbling broke out. This was new. Until now, dragons had protected Dragons' Realm. Folk sustained dragons and their riders by growing crops and providing livestock.

"I know this is not how we usually do things," said Gowp, "but we have no choice – either we fight or give in to these monsters and be slaughtered. Two folk were killed in Spanglewood settlement yesterday. We must be prepared."

Giant John strode forward, his sword in the air. "I'll train warriors."

Reina pointed at a bloody gash on his cheek. "No way," she whispered to Jerrick. I'm not doing that."

Hans held his bow high. "I need archers to ride dragons."

Master Giddi stepped closer to the fire. Shadows flickered across his soot-stained face, dancing with the dark smudges on his cheeks. His eyes gleamed and green sparks flitted from his fingers. Folk near him edged away. "We must harness magic to change the course of battle," he boomed, dark eyes flashing. "Train with me."

Jerrick elbowed Reina. "That's you."

"Too right," whispered Reina, grinning.

"More tharuks are on the move," announced Hans. "They'll be here soon. We must prepare for war."

"Everyone must choose," said Gowp, "but choose quickly."

"But Gowp," someone called, "I need my son to tend our crops."

"You won't have any crops left to tend, if we don't fight back," snapped Gowp.

The settlers' outraged cries rose.

"But the dragon riders should–"

"Why can't the wizards–"

The drummer struck twice. Folk quieted. The first streaks of dawn stole across the sky above Spanglewood Forest.

"I'll fight with Giant John," Benno called. "Who'll join us?" He gazed at Jerrick and Reina.

Giant John laid an arm over his shoulder. "Brave of you to choose first, Benno."

Reina spoke up. "Master Giddi, I'd love to train with you. Um, if that's alright."

The gangly wizard raised his bushy eyebrows and nodded. She moved to his side. His steely gaze roamed over the folk.

If Jerrick didn't choose fast, the wizard might single him out. Then he'd never be a rider. Heart pounding, Jerrick called, "Sir, ah, Hans, I've always wanted to be a dragon rider."

Hans clapped him on the back. "Just Hans, not sir. What's your name?"

"Jerrick."

"Thank you for volunteering to be our first new rider." Hans turned to the folk. "Who will ride dragons with Jerrick?"

Pa hugged Jerrick. "Good choice. I'm staying here with Giant John to protect Ma and the littlings. Fare-well your friends, then we'll go back to the family and get you ready to go."

He winked, then turned away from Jerrick and hefted his sword, bellowing, "Who will join me, Benno and Giant John to fight these monsters?"

The square was mayhem as settlers rushed to and fro. Grinning, Benno pounded Jerrick on the back. Reina ran up to Benno and hugged him, then kissed his cheek. Then she hugged and kissed Jerrick.

Beet red, Jerrick and Benno glanced at each other, then at her.

"Well," she said, hands on hips, "I'm going to miss you both."

They all grinned.

"We finally get to fight," said Benno.

"It's great," Reina said. "But it's even better that next time you two play a trick on me, I'll smite you both with wizard flame."

Jerrick hooted. "You wouldn't dare or my dragon would flame you."

Benno shook his head. "I don't envy you two. I'm glad I'm keeping my feet on the ground, right here." He flexed his muscles, already large from chopping trees beside his pa. "Someone needs to protect our families."

"You'll do a great job," said Reina.

Doubt flicked across Benno's face. "I'm not sure," he said quietly. "Those tharuks nearly killed Pa. But at least I won't end up as wizard's breakfast."

"Hopefully, neither will I," Reina shot

back.

From the looks on their faces, Jerrick knew they were all thinking the same thing: would they see each other again? "See you in battle." He stuck his fist out.

"I'm in," said Benno sticking out his fist.

"Me too," said Reina.

They all bumped fists and whooped.

Jerrick gulped. "All of us are facing risks. The whole settlement is. We have to do our best to protect our families." He gulped again thinking of Susi. "And our wee littlings."

His heart hammered. Hopefully they'd all survive.

***

You can choose which story to read next. Choose below to read your first story. At the end of the story, there will be page numbers for the other two stories, so you can see what happens to everyone. To read the stories in order, turn the page.

Warrior: Benno with Giant John
Wizard: Reina with Master Giddi
Dragon Rider: Jerrick with Hans

Read more on Amazon:

amazon.com/Eileen-Mueller/e/B00HBHSIO0

.

Free Books

By Eileen Mueller

Over a hundred and seventy dragon jokes!
Awesome Adventures!
Loads of fun!

FREE

http://www.eileenmuellerauthor.com/readers
-free-books/

ACKNOWLEDGEMENTS

Thank you to the team at Phantom Feather Press for their attention to detail. My critique partners rock – Lee Murray, A.J. Ponder, Simon Fogarty, Peter Friend, Charlotte Kieft and Michelle Child. You guys provide great feedback, awesome treats and raucous laughter as we work!

Thanks to Jan Mueller for his tireless work on the *Dragon Tales* cover – I love it. Deb Potter and Blair Polly also deserve a special mention for their support, encouragement and good humor.

Most of all, I'd like to thank my dragonets (some larger than others). Keep flying. No matter how short your wings, you can all be heroes.

Without an elusive shape-shifting harmonica player in the background, none of my work would be possible. Thank you, Kurt.

ABOUT THE AUTHOR

Eileen Mueller lives in New Zealand, on the side of a hill, with her four dragonets and a shape-shifter.

In 2014 & 2015, she had fun organizing Wellington's Storylines Family Day for thousands of kids – a festival bringing books alive through performances, crafts, and fun activities with kiwi authors and illustrators.

In her spare time, Eileen sings with Faultline, plants trees with school kids, and juggles her dragonets – usually without dropping them!

Eileen was the winner of the 2016 Sir Julius Vogel Award for best Youth Novel with Dragons' Realm. She was a finalist in the 2016 New Zealand Flash Fiction Micro Madness contest, the winner of SpecFicNZ's 2013 Going Global award and was a co-winner of NZ Society of Author's 2013 North-Write Collaboration literary award.

You can sign up for Eileen's reader's list
or find more of her books at:
EileenMuellerAuthor.com
And follow her on Amazon:

amazon.com/Eileen-Mueller/e/B00HBHSIO0

Dragon Tales Feedback

You are important. Stories are nothing without readers, so please give feedback about Dragon Tales.

This short survey will help Eileen
write stories you love:
surveymonkey.com/r/RLX7MYZ

Eileen's free books and other stories are available at:

EileenMuellerAuthor.com

Thanks for reading Dragon Tales.
Please feel free to leave a review on Amazon.

Printed in Great Britain
by Amazon

44505617R00085